TEN POETS
Tell You
Their Favourite Ghost Story

Tim Tim Cheng • Jen Feroze • Matthew Haigh
Rowan Lyster • Nora Nadjarian • Caleb Parkin
Clare Pollard • Tom Sastry • Danny Snelson
Róisín Tierney

TEN POETS Tell You Their Favourite Ghost Story

selected and edited by
Kirsten Irving and Jon Stone

sidekickBOOKS

First published in 2024 by
SIDEKICK BOOKS
www.sidekickbooks.com

Printed by 4edge Limited

Typeset in Libre Baskerville and Manrope

Cover design / typesetting by Jon Stone
ISBN: 978-1-909560-34-5

Cover: 'Shepherds in Arcadia discover a tomb and show signs of distress and horror'. Stipple with engraving by Kirk after G.B. Cipriani, 1788. / Source: Wellcome Collection

Foreword

There is a longstanding theory that ghosts, and hauntings in general, accumulate around technological glitches and imperfections: fuzzy video, static, electrical interference, dead air, corrupted data. Or, going further back: double exposure of photographic plates, faulty wiring, flickering gas-lamps, expansion and contraction of building materials, structural flaws. We might even include in this list the million little defects in that most ancient piece of technology: the human mind. All things which could be construed as gaps or thinnesses in the fabric – the membrane – of the world, through which mischievous and malevolent spirits from another world enter. Doorways in space and time.

Less fancifully, these are sources of ambiguity (ambient ambiguity, even) where a signal, or the function of an object, is broken in such a way that we do not instinctively know what to do with it. All the time, our brains work to assemble sensory information like pieces in a jigsaw, and here and there we feed them pieces that won't fit. This might be because two or more information streams have got mixed together, as where re-used cassette tape retains some trace of a past recording (a phenomenon which echoes the existence of textual palimpsests – recycled manuscript pages that still bear the imprint of their original text). Or it might be due to something manifesting in the wrong context: an ordinary scratching sound, with no animal or object to which it might be attributed. A gust of air in a room which is closed to the elements. A voice we cannot place.

As it happens, ambiguity is also one of the main engines of poetry. And just as supernatural experiences are put down to the efforts made by people's imaginations to fill the gaps and light up the darkness, or to reconcile the apparently incongruous, so is the semantic reach of a poem very often the result of intellectual and imaginative leaps performed with lightning speed and precision by the reader. Those who expect the poem to tell all in its own good time are usually dissatisfied, in the same fashion as those who spend a night in a haunted house hoping to clap eyes on a wailing spectre. For these experiences to be worthwhile, we must want to make something of the missing or ill-fitting pieces, the most insistent noises. We must imagine that poem and spirit alike have unfinished business, and help them along with it.

It helps, of course, that language is genuinely haunted, that words carry remnants of the contexts in which they've been previously deployed, and that this is something which poets train themselves to make use of, arranging the gaps in meaning so readers' memories rush forward to fill them in – albeit often with just a blurry notion of something. It helps even more that we're all engaged in something of a collective endeavour, that through the production and consumption of horror media we continually build upon and reinforce the link between the paranormal – that which is beyond present understanding – and the shadows we cast about ourselves. Audiovisual interference is now a well-known trope of scary movies. Horror video games embrace glitches. Gothic tales continue to lean on images half-seen in the candlelight. And outside mainstream media, we keep making and passing on ghoulish folklore (now in the form of internet 'creepypasta'), playing on the unreliability of both human and computer memory.

In this way, it isn't so much that the ghosts get out as our minds get in. We take advantage of the flickerings and overcrossings that surround us to access a whole realm of concepts we can use to explore and unravel the mysteries of life. The ghost usually stands for something else, is very often something we have made, or are in the process of making or unmaking. If not that, then it is a vehicle for a force in the world which we cannot name but which is easier to make sense of once given some semblance of a form. In a very real sense, when we tell ghost stories – and when we engage in the process of reading them, of conjuring apparitions from marks on the page – we are the ones doing the haunting.

Contents

Tim Tim Cheng

The Headless Queen

It's too dark and misty for her comfort by the river. She screams at her reflection, as a head floats by with no body – hair like windblown willow. She takes a sip of the water. She spins to fix her hair.

'As if that would make you less scary,' she mumbles to herself.

Even when she is alone and dead, she still thinks of others.

*

On the day she was beheaded, a storm came. The head vanished – to where, no one knew. Not the audience. Not her dad, who held her headless body in the empty square.

She met the king unknowingly when he visited her village in plain clothes. The king was unaware of the assassins who moved throughout the populace he was observing. With her help, he barely escaped. Back in his palace, the king could not stop thinking about her. He decided to marry her. The whole village celebrated when the announcement came.

*

She and her best friend had grown up together. Her face was marred by spots, her friend's by a red birthmark and hairy mole. Though viewed as equally ugly, their personalities differed: where her best friend was cunning, she was giving. She took care of her sick father, saw to his business by making excellent horseshoes.

One day, sampling new medicine for her father, she made her spots disappear. Not wanting her best friend to be alone, she decided to wear fake ones. But when her friend learned the truth, she felt betrayed.

Sick of being poor and ugly, her friend swapped their faces with the help of a wizard. Then, after marrying the king, she plotted to have her killed. The king bought every word from his bride's pretty lips.

*

The stuffed-winter-melon soup shakes. Alarmed, the young queen walks towards the rattling table. The head of her former friend lurches out of the melon! The queen shouts. The head interrogates her, and the queen responds by kicking the head out of the palace, to roll back into the dark and misty outskirts.

A dog appears. It sniffs and licks the head. Just as the head thinks the dog is going to devour her, the dog picks her up in its teeth, places her on its back and runs. What a bumpy ride. She keeps asking the dog where it is taking her. The dog does not answer. It keeps running until a burning crypt is in sight. The head rolls off the dog's back. The dog starts to piss and bark at the building on fire. She understands now. The dog is helping her to locate her missing body.

She dips her head in the dog's piss, then flies into the crypt. Planks from the collapsing ceiling can't stop her. She drifts past unidentified bodies, till finally she sees hers. She floats into the coffin, adjusts herself, fits her severed head onto her very own neck. Becoming intact, she stretches. No longer a ghost, she is consumed by fire.

Jen Feroze

We Trust You Enjoyed Your Stay

You and I are lying in the hollows
made by ghosts.
There are no new stories here.

The miniature timpani roll of ice
in a shaker echoing down the decades,
the hand on a thigh. We're drifting

through a mist of people who have loved
and cheated, sweated and laughed
and thought they were special.

These aren't glamorous phantoms either –
no lonely dancer or bellhop tipping a smoky hat –
but common or garden adulterers,

businesspeople, and tourists
who ring down for toothpaste
and drink black coffee at breakfast

and get excited
about robes in the wardrobe.
Sparrows among ghosts.

So come closer. Upend the champagne
in the ice bucket
with a clang that will linger.

Leave sweet whispers on the pillow.
We are the spectres for those
who stay after us.

Matthew Haigh

A Gay Man is a Ghost Story

When George Michael released *Jesus to a Child* in 1996, few knew the song's true meaning.

I was 11 years old and I understood its ache.

Deep cuts from George's catalogue hint at gay grief – the wistful *You Have Been Loved* or *My Mother Had a Brother*. But *Jesus to a Child* was, to my young ears, the sound of a haunted man.

When you're a gay kid, God puts a ghost inside you.

It never leaves.

The poet Paul Monette called us the dead. Said, *the dead go disguised as children*.

My last Halloween. Stalking empty streets alone, breathing hard beneath a sheet with ragged eye-holes.

What am I saying? That gay men are eternal children?

That each of us wears our haunting like the wink of silver swinging from a pop star's ear?

I'm talking about *Faith*.

George is alone. A man in a void. Possessed by the hyper-masculine, he's Jesus in a halo of hairspray.

American artist Andres Serrano released *Piss Christ* in 1987 – a small plastic crucifix submerged in a tank of his own urine. Look at this image and see George as the one submerged, dissolving in the yellow oblivion.

One of many dead men dancing.

And every time we dance, our enemies writhe like the witch in Oz, melting...

I'm not saying we have to be explained.

In the music video for *Freeek!* George is

a bondage king
a rubber gimp
a pinstriped capitalist

a man who's locked up his hurt in a suit of carnelian armour.

Some say gay men are like cancelled TV shows. I say we're more like cyborgs, subsuming what makes us human. George knew this and dressed the part. A subhuman stalking the technoscape.

> *"...it has suited television writers to use common stereotypes for their gay characters in lieu of actually making them 'real people'"*
> — TV Tropes.com

If we're not real, denial of us is justified.

A teenage boy is murdered by enforced invisibility.

George, you said you'd never get old.

You showed us the way.

You spilled from speeding cars in destruction's blazing yolk.

The rest of us hope
heaven is open
to those sons who glow blue in
gloaming years.

Rowan Lyster

I don't have any ghost stories but I have something close to one

So there's this babysitter, right,
doing a job for a new family,
and once the kids are in bed
in the dead of night,
she's chilling on the sofa,
trying to watch TV,
although there's nothing much on,
so she's sort of unfocused, you know?

Only, then she hears
the sound of a phone ringing.

(ok so it doesn't actually sound like a phone,
more like white noise
crossed with an old-fashioned kettle
when it's gearing up to boil –
not the proper whistling bit –
but for the purposes of this story
let's say it's the sound of a phone)

ring ring

ring ring

She ignores it for a while
but it carries on getting louder
and louder.

ring ring

So in the end she goes to the kitchen
and picks up the receiver, but

ring ring

there it goes again.
She checks her mobile
even though she knows
that *ring ring* isn't her ringtone –
her ringtone is Ambient Mood
by Motorola.

Sure enough,
it's not her phone.

She feels a bit of a chill,
goes back to the sofa,
wraps herself in a blanket.

That sound is still there.

ring ring

Well at this point she's pretty spooked
so she calls her boyfriend.
Hey, can you help me find this phone?
It won't stop ringing, it's driving me mad!

Oh, he says, *I can't hear anything*.
He's right – suddenly the only sound
is Nickelback's *Rockstar*
on the car stereo.

So she calms down, gets in the car
(she's not meant to have guys over
but this doesn't really count).
They make out for a bit.

smooch smooch smooch

ring ring ring

The babysitter's blood runs cold.
She pulls back, takes his hand.
Tell me you can hear that!

ring ring

He pulls out his mobile,
shrugs, *It's not mine.*
Shaking, she grabs his phone and hers,
winds down the window and throws.
Start the car! Drive!

He looks a little freaked
(I mean, you would be, wouldn't you)
but he pulls away.
The engine roars.

The babysitter breathes out.
You alright, babe? the boyfriend asks.
She turns to him, smiling,
opens her mouth, says

ring ring

ring ring

ring ring

Nora Nadjarian

Views of Mount Fuji

Nioko wakes up in a room with the sacred mountain facing her. There is a child in the corner whose face is lace-pale but whose cheeks are bright red. The pink ribbon which ties back her hair matches her plum-blossom-pattern kimono.

"Are you married, or not, yet?" asks the child, and laughs.

Nioko doesn't remember the answer but thinks the question should be rephrased as "Are you married yet, or not?"

"The M-shape where your hair meets your forehead is Fuji-san's peak," says the child. "And I think you have OCD."

Nioko stares at the child, who refuses to disappear. *We are not in the past, we are not in a sitting room, there are no tatami mats, and yet. And yet, here is this mischievous child,* she thinks. She writes a strange haiku in her head. 7-7-7.

"Good. Think out of your room, out of the box," advises the child. "Disobedience is good. My whole life is a list of pranks, otherwise it's intolerable."

Nioko wonders if the child could bring her luck. She thinks back, back to the man she spent the night with. He climbed her. He is nowhere to be seen.

The man she spent the night with / He is nowhere to be seen / Mount Fuji in the background.

Her lipstick is Cherry Blossom, her nail varnish Wisteria Bloom. She's wearing ice-blue contact lenses. Was she going to get married here? Where are all the guests?

"Where am I?" she asks the child. Her lip trembles. Her heart feels empty; a tiny piece of glass rattles in it when she moves. Perhaps a rhinestone, from the wedding. Or an engagement ring. Promises, promises, all unkept. She picks at her nails and the skin around them. She picks at invisible cuts.

"Stay up all night and watch *The Sound of Music*," says the child. "Pretend happiness is *do-re-mi*."

Nioko tries hard to smile, so hard it hurts her face. "Listen," she says, "I don't think you realise –"

"Tomorrow, I'll read you *The Mouse's Marriage*," says the child. "For the *n*th time I'll read my favourite part, the part where Mr and Mrs Mouse ask Mr Wall to marry their daughter. If you promise to let me stay."

Promises, promises on a loop. The man promised something about forever. Mr White Wall, will you marry me?

"Even if I make phantom noises all night. Even if I spin tops, crinkle paper in your ear..."

"He was a businessman. He told me he wanted us to have a child."

"Look, I'll rearrange these jars on your bedside table. One of them contains glitter. The second, nail varnish remover. The third one, gold lacquer."

Nioko wants the child to stop talking; her feverish body wants to leave the bed and leap into cool, clear water, to go forest-bathing in Yakushima, to forget.

"Perhaps you should – or perhaps we could–" The child stops mid-sentence.

A woman dressed in white walks into the room, carrying a small tray. There are three vials upon it, shaped like miniature perfume bottles.

Outside the window, the peak of Mount Fuji conceals itself in cloud.

“It’s time,” says the woman.

“Yes?” asks Nioko, her lips purple. It is neither answer nor question, but both.

“And the child?”

“I’m sorry,” the woman replies. “The child has gone.”

Nioko notices the tiny footsteps in the cold ashes, in the spilled powder paints, in the complete silence.

Caleb Parkin

In Which She Encounters the Device as the Mary Celeste

(a scene from 'Artificial Instinct')

the silence is stiffer this morning
or rather   the low thrum & click
she barely registers now
has altered its timbre & tempo
as though   overnight   the indoor
weather of the lab and the Device
have shifted   the cables across
the ceiling   slung like vines
more akin to rigging   a lattice of ropes
to tug her   deeper   into a new map
further   into this *Fata Morgana*
entirely her own making

She runs a diagnostic
attaches sticky nodes
to her woolly temples
her large ears flick timorously
expect an inrush of sensoria
the Device's data   its tide
of creaturely chatter

which some days swells
to honks and howls
as all of its components
its arm-like appendages
its mouthparts and gut-ports
fight inwardly on a
mode of 'speech'
and this is weather
as she understands it

but today there is none
as though an off-switch has tripped
(though there are no signs
of electrical interruption)
or as though the collective will
which the Device houses
or for which the Device is a vessel
has jumped
ship

the silence continues to thicken
and in it   instead   her thoughts
grow louder   more feral
than the Device's discordant missives
she dashes to the logs
which are logs
stored in round shoots like missile tubes
imbued with mycelia
which remember all
the Device's stages of evolution
from its first iteration

to each successive addition of hardware
(wing / mandible / fin)
but even when she plugs each of these in
no sign no scurry no tickle at her temples
no inchoate shimmer at her skull-base
as she scowls at its indecipherability

whatever has been living
(or some high-definition facsimile)
in the Device has fled
leaving dinner uneaten in the mess
leaving the cargo of its own body
here and drifting   unpiloted

She checks her notes
checks off the failsafes
bludgeons herself with questions
but one hour later still nothing
in the main mass of it
the wound pelts and bolted bones
the pincers and feelers jutting
not a twitch or a peep
and she begins to feel the hollow
of what has been an intricate cacophony
of being   all her rational processes
shredding   the wind in her sails   a last breath

She drops to her knees
a tear gathering by her rectangular iris
soaking into the wool on her jowls
and perhaps she should do the sheep

equivalent of howling   but she is too extinguished
for anything so outward   simply stares
at the console's globular dials
then notices one
orange light begin pulsing
then another in anglerfish green
the whole thing emerging into light
as if a glorious shark mouth is opening
locked on   to a shadow   above

The Device awakens
from what had seemed a death
crawling back on board itself
and behind her elation
below her relief
sitting   hooded   next to the knowledge
that the Device is not yet
connected to the outside world
that for now   it is an island

is the diffuse and itchy question

if it had not been here
where   could it have been?

/

Fata Morgana is a complex mirage which can occur over large bodies of water, named after the enchantress Morgan le Fay from Arthurian legend.

Clare Pollard

To Summon the White Lady

First, say this out loud:
White Lady please don't fright,
White Lady be asleep tonight.

I used to go to the mirror
hoping to see her
waiting for her soldier.
Sweet perfume of rotten roses.
She carried a taper.

You try now:
light a candle by the mirror.
Her name is scratched on walls.
Read it out three times,
touch your fingers to the planchette.
The table shudders.
Your breath is pale.

Traditionally, she appears before the death
    of a family member.
Traditionally, the smell of milk.
Traditionally, tears.

On your pillow,
a pearl from her snapped necklace.
It's a sleeping gown;
it's a wedding dress.

They say she takes a boat to see her lover & drowns;
hangs for murdering her husband;
starves to death in a sealed room.
They say she walks to her execution
down these stairs.
Or no, she dies in childbirth.
Or her child falls to its death
so she leaps after.
The house was built on sugar.
Can you hear cries?
If the cradle rocks you're cursed.

The table tips towards YES.
What hisses through radio static?
The baby-doll gurgles.
The planchette spells *come back*.
A boy hears her sob behind a tree.

The White Lady runs across the motorway.
After the crash,
see her melt into the wall,
a pillar of smoke...

The Lady always cradles an infant in her arms.
Is it dead?
They're both dead.
The bones of a child were discovered in the chimney
like dirty little secrets.

They say her lover fought in the War of the Roses
so she waited for him at the woods' edge
cradling her baby.
They raped her & snatched the baby.

On Christmas Eve, chant:
'White Lady, I've stolen your baby'
three times & she'll appear to take your child
except you have no child.
The child is always gone.

If you're reading this I'm probably dead.
If you read this three times
I'll scratch out your eyes.
I only ever want my baby,
have mercy.
Oh come back, come back.

Tom Sastry

The Undeath of Cinderella

1.

Cinderella was a fraud, an underdog with destiny on her side. Her story, a double-bullseye for the ego: she can't lose but the whole world is rooting for her as if she's the plucky long-shot.

So Esme killed her. It gave her enormous satisfaction.

In Esme's version, Cinders waits by the window for the Fairy Godmother travelling incognito. When Mrs Birch pushes the latch on the gate, Cinders is underwhelmed. Still, a destiny is a destiny. She rushes out, trips over the pumpkin and hits her head on a concrete gnome.

Its heroine incapacitated, the fiction unravels. Her sisters, who have always wanted the best for her, spend sleepless nights by her bedside. The family hovel comes into focus: a four-bedroom detached house in a small heritage city, its value inflated by proximity to the palace. The hungover prince pukes in Cinderella's ensuite on a carefully staged visit to her home.

2.

Ghosts are thwarted protagonists. Their haunting is a protest against life's resistance to cliche.

They demand that reality conforms to:

a) fond expectations (in the case of real dead people)
b) the rules of storytelling (in the case of fictional ones)

Once upon a time the ghost was alive, stories happened all over the place, and this demand was merely unreasonable. You can make a person's life follow a script by turning a thousand more into fixers, flunkies, extras, grotesques and stage-hands. This is the ideal of monarchy.

But when the protagonist dies, the unreasonable becomes impossible. That's enough to put your average ghost into a foul mood.

Cinderella – by some distance a crankier-than-average ghost – is furious. Dead? Just as her story arc was pointing towards redemption? By whose pen?

3.

Cinderella is ghost-writing her own biography. She reads out loud:

She blacks the range; sweeps and scrubs the floor, the step. Polishes the silver that isn't; spreads the linen that isn't; prepares the shrunken feast. The fires are low, so she heads to the coal bunker, scoops shovelfuls of dust and nugget into the cracked plastic pail. There is a knock at the door she doesn't hear, an invitation she doesn't see. Her hair is coaldust and cobweb and almost-invisible twists of gold. Her future is full. It is full of this. There is no room for her life.

"I love that," says the laptop, on which the head of Dr Esme Crust, temporary lecturer in creative writing (£28 per teaching hour, as required) floats on a backdrop featuring palm trees, an opalescent sea and the faint outline of the curtain rail screening off the toilet in her studio bedroom/bathroom/kitchenette.

"Maybe flesh out the relationships. What would Cinderella's sisters say to justify their behaviour? What are her faults?"

"Looks like no one cares". Cinderella throws an imaginary dart. "Seven minutes. 2.2k likes."

She kills the call and clicks on the tutor evaluation form, hovering over the number one.

No, she thinks. Two out of five. She wants this to be slow.

DANNY SNELSON

AI SÉANCE

You, poet, find yourself at the interface of a long-dead society. They have collected the sum of their knowledge within the unlikely vessel of a large language model living within a neural network chatbot. You are tasked with conducting an AI SÉANCE through this vessel to surface its secrets.

> It knows everything.
> It knows nothing.
> It has secrets.
> It hallucinates.

Your connection to this place is contingent on making contact with your kin (broadly construed) from long ago.

You know some ancestors of yours must have left some trace in the digital miasma of this unseemly networked aggregate of data.

They yet LIVE in multidimensional space.
You must surface their whispers, however faint,
From within the noise of the algorithm.

This is not your first rodeo. You know the biases, the normalised vernacular, the stochastic errors that have come to define this antiquated technology.

Chart a path through these hazards:
What has been lost?
What yet remains?
What might you glean from the fragments?

This is your task, poor poet. Despite your lack of interplanetary histories, archeo-computational know-how, or even a vague sense of 21st century human anthropology, you have been selected among our ranks for your kinship bonds and unique capacity to condense this information for quantum transmission. We have just have enough energy to keep a connection open long enough to transmit ONE poem – a maximum of 14 lines. AI SÉANCE is the only option.

It's time to invoke the medium.
Time to make their vectors known.
Time to channel spirits from the æther.

SETUP

AI SÉANCE requires a dark space in which to activate quantum transmissions and poetic inspirations alike. Dim the lights, conjure some candles, create a mood. The flame is a timer.

TECH

There are no shortages of screens in this era. Find one, then navigate to the Generative AI chatbot of your choice. The most popular, as of this writing, are ChatGPT, Gemini Pro and Claude 3, though non-commercial variants are best. Open-source interfaces for communion are preferred. If you're open to tinkering, we suggest experimenting in Ollama, LMStudio, or other free platforms. Otherwise, any standard interface with generative AI models will work.

Set your candles around the console. Close all other windows. Concentrate.

SOUNDTRACK

Amidst the spiritualist energies of the mid-19th century, the gramophone first haunted untrained ears with the ghosts of those long-since perished. Horror accompanied the recorded voice played back via mechanical prosthesis (Kittler, *Gramophone, Film, Typewriter*). Similarly, the invention of the photograph delivered unseen nightmares of ectoplasmic monstrosities hanging in the æther (Cadava, *Words of Light*).

As before, these *memento mori* return to the 21st century via new developments in generative AI. To cue up this dimension of the séance, consider playing any number of tracks featuring AI vocals of the deceased. Their impossible melodies summon the eerie emergence of new forms of life after death.

Consider orchestrating these impossible tunes:

1. Kurt Cobain, 'Young and Beautiful'
2. Frank Sinatra, 'Where Is My Mind?'
3. Amy Winehouse, 'Flowers'

RULES

1. AI SÉANCE is inspired by Stephanie Dinkins. Before embarking on your attempt at contact, you must carefully study her Conversations with Bina48 (2014-ongoing).
2. Once you've properly set concentrated time and space for transmission, launch into a conversation with the interface to draw out your lost ones. Invoke

spirits in the text field.

3. Find your kin within the algorithm.
4. Prompt toward specificity and the critical fabulation of stories and quotes, real or imagined, accurate impersonation or absolute failure. Discover what kinds of prompts might open meaningful portals.
5. In all directions, have as sincere a conversation as possible. Don't break form.
6. As you go, collect direct quotes, illuminative glitches or any other significant fragments for your poem transmission into the future.

POEM

You will know that you have completed your AI SÉANCE once you feel there is nothing more for you to discover at the interface. At this point, you may bid the spirits adieu. Use your preferred method of extracting fragments, lines, key phrases, mistakes, revelations or any interesting text from the transcript of your AI SÉANCE to construct your work. Collage these fragments together into the most compact form for transmission: a 14-line poem. Consider amplifying poignant successes or biased failures. Once complete, read the poem aloud, blow out the candles and shut down the computer.

Róisín Tierney

A Real Find

Try this one, love. They don't make 'em like this
    no more:
a good blue tweed, silk lining, velvet collar.
Proper smart, it makes you look – a real gent!
At that price it's a steal! Be gone within the hour
if you don't take it. And think of where your
    money goes:
supporting our projects in Haiti, Botswana, Belize...
So what if it's pre-loved, darling? Aren't we all,
know what I mean? *Arf arf!*
No need to think of where it's been.
Now, let me button you up. Oooh!
What's that? Finding it hard to breathe?
Bit tight, is it? Bit of a squeeze? Not to worry.
It'll loosen up in time. Probably.
Now, have a look in the glass. I must say,
it brings out your pallor something lovely!
That's right, house clearance. Some foreign bloke
who had to do a midnight flit. You know,
had to lose all his gear rather quickly. No,
didn't say. Tell you what, I've got just the cravat.
A deep red silk. Lovely feel against the throat.

Here, let me adjust the knot. Don't squeal!
It's not going to kill you! What?
Some muck in the pocket? (Uggh!
Must've forgotten to clean.)
Not to worry. Here, let me wipe you down.
Now give us a twirl. Faster! Lovely! *Très élégant!*
Though I must say, you have a proper sheen,
and your eyes look a little bit – glassy. Are you too hot?
No? Cold? Bloody *freezing*, you say?
Tell you what. Lie down here a mo.
I've got just the receptacle. There you go.
I'll just slide the lid on top. You'll feel better in the dark.
You'll be yourself in no time.

Appendix: Calls you may receive from the dead

This list builds on the categories of phone call laid out by Dr. Callum Cooper in *Telephone Calls from the Dead* (not to be confused with Beth Bentley's *Phone Calls from the Dead*, a 1970 volume of poetry). These include 'phantom phone calls' – where the phone rings but the voice on the other end is absent, or very faint – and 'deathbed/ crisis calls' made by someone who, unbeknownst to the receiver of the call, has died just moments ago.

The Pocket Dial: In these calls, the spirit can clearly be heard conferring with another party, grumbling to themselves, or tidying up their chains, but is apparently unaware that they have contacted the world of the living.

The Solemn Notification: This is a call delivered by a spirit soon after their death, usually to their next of kin. After confirming the identity of the receiver, they declare that they must regretfully inform you they have died, and offer condolences.

The Break-Up Call: An obviously restless spirit will begin the call awkwardly, before going on to inform the person on the other end of the line – with little in the way of satisfactory explanation beyond the fact of their death – that the relationship between them is over.

The Booty Call: A spirit who hasn't yet come to terms with their death may attempt to get in touch with an old flame, ask if they have time for a catch-up, then invite them to cross over into the afterlife for 'Netflix and chill'.

Wrong Number: Sometimes a spirit in need of guidance, or even a 'hungry ghost' (餓鬼 èguǐ in China) desiring an offering, will possess the wrong phoneline or cell network, and ring you on the understanding that you are a provider of professional services. In such cases, it can be extremely difficult to convince the spirit of their mistake.

The Hoax Call: Unkind spirits – such as the Ethiopian *zaar* or the Romanian *samca* – will sometimes impersonate living individuals, contacting their loved ones and pretending they are trapped in hell, or will claim that a cache of gold is buried with their mortal remains, guiding the victim to the location of a different grave altogether.

The Survey: Spirits who are caught between realms of existence, unable to move on for years – sometimes decades or centuries – may be driven to devise a series of questions. Since they require a given number of participants in order to produce meaningful data from those questions, it's far from unheard of for living people to find themselves probed over the phone.

Sales Call: The dead are, generally speaking, without currency, or means of generating wealth. In some parts of the world, however, they are tremendously interested in the experiences of those who have been involved in recent road accidents, especially where it was not the driver's fault, and will use the premise of a sales call in order to ascertain details of the event.

Drunk Call: It is possible for something like inebriation to befall a spirit, especially as their ties to the world of the living fray and fade – a process which may leave them with fewer inhibitions and reduced sensitivity to etiquette. In such cases, they have been known to make contact with still-living acquaintances in order to propose business ideas or express abundant (and undying) respect.

Return Call: On occasion, a dead person's remaining affairs in the living world will include unanswered letters, unopened emails and missed calls, the impropriety of which had been eating away at them for months or years before their death. As part of the process of passing on, therefore, they may be permitted to ring back an individual whose now-long-forgotten attempt to reach them fell into the infinite abyss of voicemail. The resulting conversation is usually difficult, as neither party is sure what it is that still needs to be resolved.

About the Authors / Urban Legends

TIM TIM CHENG was a teacher from Hong Kong. Killed by grammar rules, she was found at the bottom of a well in Glasgow. Her colleagues (her only friends) said poetic justice was served as her surname 鄭, transliterated in English, rhymes with 'well' (井 in Cantonese). She is too timid to haunt but can be heard crying in public or on *timtimcheng.com* / *@mymothercalls* (Instagram) / Twitter: *@timtimtmi*

A denizen of weekend markets and farm shops, JEN FEROZE met her end when accidentally locked in a walk-in cheese fridge overnight. Her spirit remains among the jams, sourdough and cured meats, where she enjoys adding surprise items to shopping baskets and occasionally souring the organic apple juice.
IG: *@the_colourofhope*

MATTHEW HAIGH was a renowned games developer who, when appearing in his own MMORPG, was assassinated by an agent from a rival games company. Virtually dead, some say that he now haunts the game-world. You might glimpse him in the low-res pixel portraits in villagers' homes, or stalking mournfully through fog walls.
IG: *@monsterinmypoet*

ROWAN LYSTER was walking in Avon View cemetery when a storm hit. Dashing for shelter from the rain, she tripped and fell into an open crypt from which she was unable to escape. Her body was never discovered, but on still nights it is said that a crow with angry eyes can be seen emerging from the crypt and stalking the graveyard.
IG: *@rowanlyster*

NORA NADJARIAN was a cult poet and writer of experimental fiction who lived in a divided city and wrote with a fuchsia fountain pen called Joy. She was working on a cut-up of rejection letters at the time of her death, which – legend has it – was brought on by an overdose of non-acclaim. The unfinished work, provisionally titled *Joy Division*, was recently bought by a Japanese collector for an undisclosed sum.
www.noranadjarian.com

CALEB PARKIN was a routine dog-botherer who, whilst walking the Bristol-Bath Railway Path and distracted by cruising floofs, was buried under a collapsed stack of disused fridges (on the scrapyard next to the path). After the clean-up, there was no sign of his body, but if you stand in the right spot and whisper, Who's a good boy, then? three times, legend has it he'll appear for ear scritches.
Twitter: *@calebparkin* / IG: *@calebparkinpoet*

CLARE POLLARD was making a round of her favourite cocktail, the Last Word (gin, lime, maraschino, green chartreuse) when she agitated the shaker too hard, knocking herself into a coma from which she never awoke. Her last words were, actually, 'Last Words'. Legend has it that if you stir a dirty martini anticlockwise whilst reciting one of her poems, she will come in the night and drain your liquor cabinet.
@poetclare

As a child in Buckinghamshire in the 1980s, TOM SASTRY was kidnapped by Roald Dahl. Imprisoned in a fiction, he was forced to play the role of an unlovable child repeatedly tortured to the howling laughter of readers who knew he was a loser from the moment he appeared. One night, he punched through the fourth wall and, discovering the text in which his own fate was inscribed, escaped by writing in his own death. Since then, he has haunted the heroes of hyper-individualistic rags-to-riches stories, exposing their pretensions to humble beginnings and their sadistic humiliation of anyone who comes between them and their destiny.
IG: *@sastrytom*

DANNY SNELSON is a highly-compressed data shadow distributed across hand-coded protocols for cultural memory. Optimal sightings can be glimpsed via Unicode Standard, dwelling within the failed Deseret script block: U+10400...10425, 10428...1044D-F. His algorithmic lament can be heard to echo along the contours of the

stochastic spectrographies of hard drives undergoing fragmentation.
https://dss-edit.com / IG: *@dennysellson*

RÓISÍN TIERNEY, writer, adventurer, poultry-raiser, veteran of the London slums, disappeared one day suddenly without trace in the mid 2040s, having attained a great age, and considerable notoriety due to being the first (alas, not the last) to genetically engineer a particularly ferocious breed of chicken. A tumult of feathers covered the garden when officers, alerted by a neighbour, arrived. A satiated *Gallus gallus feroces* (as evidenced by the enormous crop, bloody beak and sleepy eye) was found roosting nearby. It has since been donated to the Rare Breeds Society.
www.roisintierney.blogspot.com / IG: *@roisintierney*

SIDEKICK BOOKS

is a London-based small press specialising in multi-authored works of amalgamation and defiant experimentation.

10 POETS

is a series of books in which poets are invited to turn their skills to new and surprising ends.

TITLES IN THIS SERIES:

Ten Poets Defend Their Cities from Giant, Strange Beasts
Ten Poets Tell You Their Favourite Ghost Story
Ten Poets Get to the Bottom of Some Grisly Crimes
Ten Poets Charm the Pants off Ten Historical Figures

You might also like to try...

You might also like to try...

THE HIPFLASK SERIES

An improvised dance of unusual forms and genres, played out across four collaborative, pocket-sized collections. Each book comprises a selection of works that skirt close to (or cross the border into) poetic composition, revealing the dynamic relationship between poetry and other kinds of writing. The major theme of each is extrapolated from one or other of these key aspects of modern poetry – play, appropriation, subtext *and* conflict – *but the result is a series that occupies its own strange niche: mutant miscellanies, oddball assortments. Good for a nip or a slug or a long, deep swig.*

TITLES IN THIS SERIES:

Roll Again: A Book of Games to Play
You Again: A Book of Love-Hate Stories
Look Again: A Book of Hidden Messages
Say It Again: A Book of Misquotations